The FARMYARD CAT

Christine Anello

illustrated by Sharon Thompson

SCHOLASTIC INC.

New York Toronto London Auckland Sydney

For Frank and Joseph Errol

ISBN 0-590-42852-7

All rights reserved. Published by Scholastic Inc.,
730 Broadway, New York, NY 10003, by arrangement with
Ashton Scholastic Pty, Inc.

12 11 10 9 8 7 6 5   6 7 8 9/9 0/0

Printed in the U.S.A.   08

First Scholastic printing, October 1990

The farmyard cat was out walking. She was very, very, hungry.

She spied the big fat chickens
in the farmyard hen-house.

'I'll get you, chickens!'
hissed the cat.
'I'll get you!'
She sprang high
and clung on to
the hen-house wire.

But . . . down bent the wire,
and down fell the farmyard cat.

With claws stretched w-i-d-e,
she landed . . .

. . . on top of the farmyard dog.

The farmyard dog was very angry.
He began to chase the farmyard cat.

'I'll get you, cat!' growled the dog.
'I'll get you!'

The farmyard dog chased the farmyard cat
under the paddock fence.

They woke . . .

. . . the farmyard bull.

The farmyard bull was very angry.
He began to chase the farmyard cat.

'I'll get you, cat!' bellowed the bull.
'I'll get you!'

The farmyard bull
charged through
the paddock fence.

SMASH

The fence broke!

The animals disturbed . . .

. . . the farmyard nanny-goat.

The farmyard nanny-goat
was very angry.
She began to chase
the farmyard cat.

'I'll get you, cat!'
bleated the goat.
'I'll get you!'

The animals raced through the grassy paddock.

The farmyard cat ran through the legs . . .

. . . of the farmyard horse.

The farmyard horse was very angry.
He began to chase the farmyard cat.

'I'll get you, cat!'
snorted the horse.
'I'll get you!'

The animals were going too fast!
Suddenly . . .

. . . the farmyard cat stopped!

The farmyard animals
fell over the farmyard cat.
The farmyard animals
fell over each other.

They fell . . .

. . . into the muddy sty
  of the farmyard pigs.

The farmyard cat
looked at all the muddy animals.
'How very clever I am!' she mewed.

The farmyard cat walked proudly away,
with her tail in the air.

'I got you animals.
I got you!' she purred.

'I got you ALL!'